This book belongs to:

_____

To Alexandra. Now the secret's out! With love D.R

For Maya, H.S.

IS DADDY HOME YET?

Dean Russell &
Harry Sankey

"Mummy, is Daddy home yet?
        Will he be back before bed?
Or perhaps when our
        night-time story's been read?"

"Oh honey, I told you. He called, he'll be late.
He is stuck in some traffic.
He'll be home before 8!"

"So, he'll give you a **cuddle** and a **big kiss** goodnight when you're sound asleep later. Now let's turn out the light."

'But why is he late?'
- thought the child in bed...

...imagining reasons of 'why' in his head.

Could it be traffic
in a spectacular race,
in a fantastical spaceship
at incredible pace?

Look at those aliens as they crash into stars!

That's it, 'yes, go Daddy', you're almost at Mars.

He's done it and won it

at a **splendiferous** rate.

Hooray for my Daddy!

No wonder he's late...

"Mummy?" said the child
after some minutes more

"Is Daddy not home yet?

Are you certain?

Are you sure?"

"Oh honey,
he just called.
He's trying
his best.

He's stuck
in a jam.
Now please
try to rest."

'But why is he 'stuck in the jam'?' - thought the child in his bed...

...imagining reasons of 'why' in his head.

Perhaps he is hiding in a big giant's lair.
He's trapped in the kitchen,
on a shelf right up there.

His foot is all **squelchy**
from the jam he ran through.

Now he's made it to the bathroom and **jumped** down the loo.

He did it, he made it! He really is ace.

(Even if he smells bad from his daring escape!)

"Mummy?" said the boy.
After just ten minutes more.
"Is Daddy not home yet?
Are you certain? Are you sure?"

"Daddy's not home yet.
he's running behind.
Now just go to sleep please.
if you don't mind."

'But why is he running' -
thought the child in the bed,
imagining reasons of
'why' in his head.

perhaps it's from **pirates**...

...on a ship far from shore.

Oh no! I see **Blackbeard**...

...chasing Dad with his **Sword**!

But Daddy's not frightened.
as he swings on the sail.

He pushes old **Blackbeard**,
into the mouth of a **whale!**

He's done it, he swung it!

What an amazing shipmate.

Hooray for my Daddy!

No wonder he's late.

As the child's eyes grow heavy,

he falls asleep for the night –

not hearing the footsteps

so incredibly light.

Slowly, Daddy's head peeps round the boy's door,
and gives a kiss and a hug
as the child dreams some more...

The End

First published in Great Britain in 2013 by
Far Far Away Books and Media Ltd,
20-22 Bedford Row, London, WC1R 4JS

ISBN: 978-1-908786-78-4
A CIP catalogue record for this book is available from the British Library.

Designed at www.aitchcreative.co.uk

Edited by Richard Trenchard

Printed and bound in Portugal by Printer Portuguesa.

All Far Far Away Books can be ordered from
www.centralbooks.com

www.farfarawaybooks.com